Isabelle's New Friend

A Random House PICTUREBACK®

Library of Congress Cataloging-in-Publication Data:
Brunhoff, Laurent de, 1925-   . Isabelle's new friend : a Babar book / by Laurent de Brunhoff.   p.   cm. – (A Random House picture-back) SUMMARY: Isabelle the elephant and Vic the rhino persist in their controversial friendship despite the bad feelings between their respective species.   ISBN: 0-394-82880-1 (pbk.); 0-394-92880-6 (lib. bdg.)   [1. Elephants–Fiction. 2. Rhinoceros–Fiction. 3. Prejudices–Fiction] I. Title.   PZ7.B82843Is   1989   [E]–dc19   89-3727

Manufactured in the United States of America   1 2 3 4 5 6 7 8 9 0

Laurent de Brunhoff

Isabelle's New Friend

Random House 🏠 New York

It was a beautiful day. Babar and his family were having a
cookout. Suddenly Cornelius spotted a little rhino!

"What are you doing here?" Cornelius shouted. But he got no
answer. The little rhino ran away.

"Why did Cornelius yell at that little rhino?" Isabelle asked her mother that evening.

"Long ago there was a war with the rhinos," said Celeste. "Cornelius thinks all rhinos are bad–big or small."

Isabelle did not think that was so. She thought the little rhino looked nice. The next day she went looking for him. And there he was!

"Hi!" she said. "I am Isabelle."

"And I am Vic," he told her.

Isabelle and Vic had lots of fun together.

Isabelle told silly stories. Vic whistled like a bird.

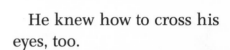

He knew how to cross his eyes, too.

"I wish I could do that," Isabelle said, laughing.

Then Vic said, "Let's go to Rhino City. You can meet all my friends."

So off they went.

In Rhino City everyone stared at Isabelle. They whispered to each other. "An elephant in Rhino City? How *very* strange!"

Lady Rataxes was terribly angry.

"You cannot be friends with that little elephant," she told her son.

King Rataxes ordered Isabelle to leave at once.

"And don't come back again. We don't like elephants in Rhino City," he shouted.

Isabelle walked back to Celesteville. She felt so sad. Would she ever see her new friend again?

Vic was unhappy too. The very next day he sneaked out of Rhino City and went looking for Isabelle.

Isabelle had the same idea. And it was not long before they ran into each other.

"Hooray!" they shouted. "Let's go play!"

Vic showed Isabelle a boat.

"My father and I like to go fishing," said Vic. "Do you want to go for a ride?"

"That would be fun," said Isabelle.

Soon they were in the middle of the lake.
"Look, there's an island." Isabelle pointed. "Can we land there?"
"Why not?" said Vic.

Isabelle and Vic hurried ashore.
"Let's go exploring," said Vic.
"Follow me."

Isabelle and Vic played toss-the-coconut and
hide-and-seek.

Suddenly a strong wind started to blow. The sky grew dark and it started raining. Isabelle and Vic ran back to the boat. But when they got to the shore, the boat was gone!

"How will we ever get home?" cried Isabelle as they ran along the shore, searching for the lost boat.

"Don't worry, Isabelle," said Vic, trying to sound brave. "You are my friend. I won't let anything bad happen to you. We'll find the boat."

"Oh, look!" cried Vic. "There it is!"
"Mister, Mister!" Isabelle shouted. "That's our boat."

"I know you," the hippo told Isabelle. "You're Babar's little girl. I'm Murphy Heavybottom."

"Now I remember you," Isabelle said. "And this is my friend Vic."

"Nice to meet you, Vic," Murphy replied. "Hop aboard and I'll tow you back to the mainland."

The hippo took Isabelle and Vic back to his house. It was a pretty house with a large balcony. Madame Heavybottom was there to welcome them.

"You need to dry off," she said. "Then we will call your parents so they will not worry."

Madame Heavybottom gave them towels. Isabelle pretended hers was a long, flowing gown.
"I am queen," she told Vic.
"Then I must be king," said Vic.

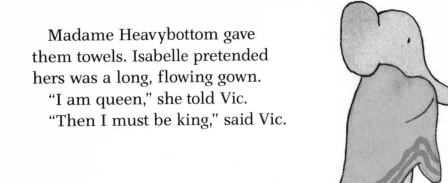

When the sun came out, they hung their clothes up to dry. Murphy gave them a telescope.
"I can see Celesteville from here," said Vic.

There was a water slide on the side of the house. Isabelle and Vic took turns.

"Let's see who can make the biggest splash," said Vic.

"Me first." Isabelle laughed. And down she went.

Whoooosh!

Then the hippo came to the window. "Come inside," he called. "It's time to go."

"I have tried to call your parents," said Murphy. "But there is no answer. I will have to take you home myself."

"First we will go to Rhino City, then to Celesteville," the hippo told the two friends. And off they went.

They had not gone far when Isabelle said, "Wait! I think I hear voices!"
"Who could it be?" asked Vic.
"Let's go find out," said Murphy.

It was Babar and Rataxes! Celeste and Lady Rataxes were there too. Everyone had been out looking for the children.

"What have you done with Vic?" shouted Rataxes.
"I bet he is with Babar's daughter!" said Lady Rataxes.
Babar shook his head angrily. "I have no idea where Vic is," he explained. "I am looking for Isabelle, and I'm as worried as you are."

The children ran to their parents.
"Here we are!" they cried.

"Thank you so much for bringing the children back safely," Babar said to Murphy.

But Lady Rataxes was still angry.

"Maybe now your daughter will stay away from our son!"

"Let's get home now," said Babar. Then he climbed into his car and drove off toward Celesteville. Isabelle waved to her friend, and Vic waved back as Rataxes headed for Rhino City.

Isabelle could not stop thinking about her friend.

"Do you think I'll ever see Vic again?" Isabelle asked her father that evening.

"I hope so," said Babar. "He is a nice little boy."

Sure enough, the very next day there was a tap at the window.
Guess who it was!
"My friend!" cried Isabelle.
Then she ran out to play.